AN ELGAR FLUTE ALI

GW00504240

FLUTE

CANTO POPOLARE

from *In the South*

Molto tranquillo ♩. =56

pp molto espress.

dim.

quasi ad lib.

dim.   *dim.*   *dim.*

p

dolce

dolce

mf sonore

p   *p dolce*

pp   *p*

rall.

pp   *dolce*   *dim. molto*   *ppp*

THE TAME BEAR

from *The Wand of Youth, Second Suite*

MINUET

from *The Wand of Youth, First Suite*

THEME

from Symphony No. 1

SERENADE

from *The Wand of Youth, First Suite*

MOTHS AND BUTTERFLIES

from *The Wand of Youth, Second Suite*

THEME AND TWO VARIATIONS

from *Enigma Variations*

VARIATION VIII

VARIATION IX

CHANSON DE MATIN

Trinty G6
B piece

8

CHANSON DE NUIT

2/10 (172706)

An Elgar Flute Album

Arranged by Trevor Wye

Piano Accompaniments by Robert Scott

GRADE IV-VI

Novello

Cover by Art & Design Services

CONTENTS

AN ELGAR FLUTE ALBUM

CANTO POPOLARE

from *In the South*

Arranged by
TREVOR WYE

4

THE TAME BEAR
from *The Wand of Youth, Second Suite*

MINUET

from *The Wand of Youth, First Suite*

THEME

from Symphony No. 1

SERENADE

from *The Wand of Youth, First Suite*

12

MOTHS AND BUTTERFLIES

from *The Wand of Youth, Second Suite*

16

THEME AND TWO VARIATIONS

from *Enigma Variations*

VARIATION VIII
W. N.

VARIATION IX
Nimrod

CHANSON DE MATIN

24

CHANSON DE NUIT

Music for Flute

Solo

Gordon Saunders
Eight Traditional Japanese Pieces
Gordon Saunders has selected and transcribed these pieces for tenor recorder solo or flute from the traditional folk music of Japan.

Trevor Wye
Practice Book for the Flute
Volume 1 TONE
Volume 2 TECHNIQUE
Volume 3 ARTICULATION
Volume 4 INTONATION
Volume 5 BREATHING AND SCALES

Flute & Piano

Richard Rodney Bennett
Summer Music *Associated Board Grade VII*

Charles Camilleri
Sonata Antica

Edward Elgar
An Elgar Flute Album *arranged by Trevor Wye*

Gabriel Fauré
A Fauré Flute Album *arranged by Trevor Wye*

James Galway
Showpieces
The Magic Flute of James Galway
Two albums, each containing ten favourite pieces by various composers, arranged for flute and piano by James Galway. Both include photographs and a separate flute part.

Michael Hurd
Sonatina

John McCabe
Portraits *Associated Board Grades V & VI*

Eric Satie
A Satie Flute Album *arranged by Trevor Wye*

Robert Schumann
A Schumann Flute Album *arranged by Trevor Wye*

Gerard Schurmann
Sonatina

604(85)

Trevor Wye

Tutors

A Beginner's Book for the Flute   Part 1
                                         Part 2
                                         Piano Accompaniment

Practice Books for the Flute   Volume 1   TONE
                                            Volume 2   TECHNIQUE
                                            Volume 3   ARTICULATION
                                            Volume 4   INTONATION AND VIBRATO
                                            Volume 5   BREATHING AND SCALES

Arrangements for Flute & Piano

An Elgar Flute Album
A Fauré Flute Album
A Satie Flute Album
A Schumann Flute Album

Mozart Flute Concerto in G K.313
Mozart Flute Concerto in D K.314 and Andante in C K.315

611(86)